D0859293

"Hop into bed," said Mother as she turned off the light,
"and I'll tell you what I know about fairies."

So begins a whimsical journey through the magic and mystery of the fairy world, where marvelous winged creatures paint rainbows, teach birds to sing, hang stars in the evening sky, and welcome children to dreamland. Best-selling author-illustrator team Kathleen and Michael Hague open a door to a fantastic realm of fairies in a good-night journey that will inspire both parent and child.

Be sure to look for the red-capped fairy hidden on every page!

Kathleen Hague

Illustrated by Michael Hague

Good Night, Fairies

chronicle books · san francisco

To Devon

First paperback edition published in 2007 by Chronicle Books LLC.

Text © 2002 by Kathleen Hague.
Illustrations © 2002 by Michael Hague.
All rights reserved.

Book design by Nicole Stanco de las Heras.
Typeset in Cochin and Tagliente.
The illustrations in this book were rendered in pen and ink, watercolor, and colored pencils.
Manufactured in China.

ISBN 978-0-8118-5762-8

The Library of Congress has catalogued the previous edition as follows:
Hague, Kathleen
Good night, fairies / by Kathleen Hague; illustrated by Michael Hague.
p. cm.
Summary: At bedtime, a mother tells her curious child about the things that fairies do,
like hang stars in the evening sky and care for toys that children have lost.
ISBN 1-58717-134-1
[1. Fairies—Fiction. 2. Bedtime—Fiction. 3. Mother and child—Fiction.]
I. Hague, Michael, ill. II. Title.
PZ7.H1246 Go 2002   [E]—dc21   2001049867

10 9 8 7 6 5 4 3

Chronicle Books LLC
680 Second Street, San Francisco, California 94107

www.chroniclekids.com

"It's time for bed," said Mother.

"I was wondering," said the child.

"About what?" asked Mother.

"About fairies."

"Hop into bed," said Mother as she turned off the light,
"and I'll tell you what I know about fairies."

"What do the fairies do when it's nighttime?"
asked the child.

"Well, the fairies hang the stars in the evening sky,"
answered Mother, "so every child will have

a night-light."

"Why?" asked the child.

"Because fairies love little children like you,"
said Mother. "Of all the world's creatures,
there is nothing so like a fairy as a child."
"Do fairies have toys?" asked the child.
"Fairies don't have toys of their own, but they gather
and care for all of the toys children have lost,"
answered Mother.

"Do fairies ever sleep?" asked the child.

"On leafy beds in secret gardens," said Mother.

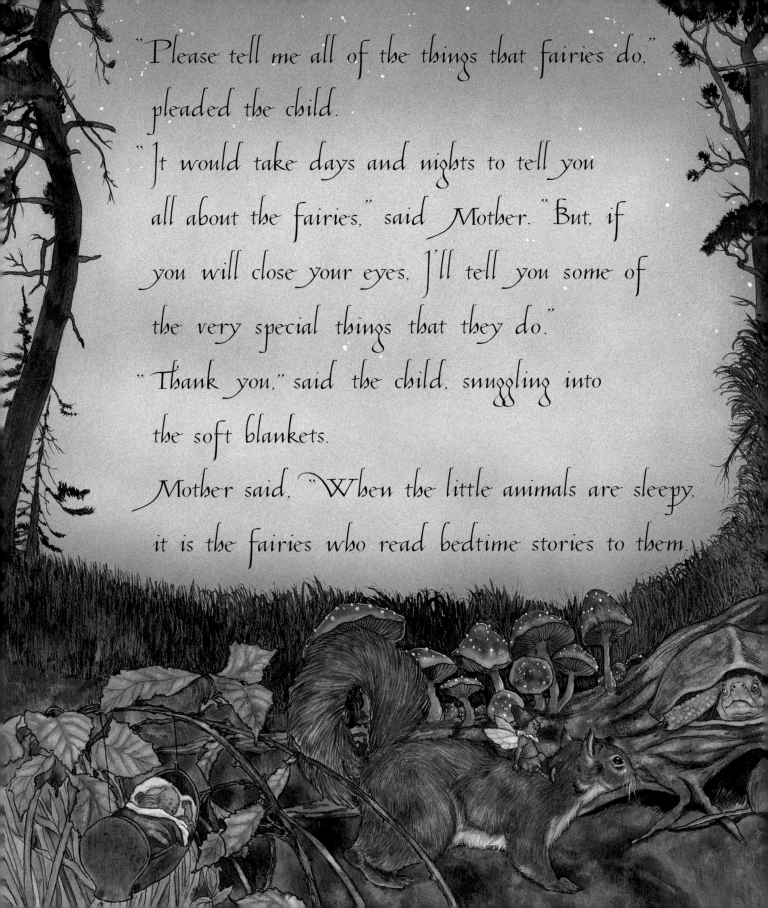

"Please tell me all of the things that fairies do," pleaded the child.

"It would take days and nights to tell you all about the fairies," said Mother. "But, if you will close your eyes, I'll tell you some of the very special things that they do."

"Thank you," said the child, snuggling into the soft blankets.

Mother said, "When the little animals are sleepy, it is the fairies who read bedtime stories to them."

Other fairies paint the wings of tiny bugs
and make the butterflies beautiful.

There are fairies who teach the birds to sing . . .

...and the unicorns to fly.

It is the fairies who comb the mermaids' hair . . .

...and draw rainbows to brighten rainy days.

It is the fairies who scatter the autumn leaves

and paint the winter world white.

Fairies make the spring flowers bloom.

And on warm summer nights they dress in
spiders' lace and dance to the twilight orchestra.

And when little ones close their eyes and go to sleep,
it is the fairies who welcome them to dreamland."

"Good night," whispered Mother. But the child was already far, far away.

Can you find and count all 321 winged fairies in this book?
Don't forget to look at the endpapers!

Kathleen and Michael Hague are the creators of several best-selling books, including *Ten Little Bears*, *Alphabears*, and *Numbears*. Michael Hague has also illustrated numerous popular editions of children's classics, including *The Tale of Peter Rabbit* and *The Nutcracker* (both available from Chronicle Books), *Peter Pan*, *The Wizard of Oz*, *The Velveteen Rabbit*, and *The Secret Garden*. He is also the author and illustrator of *Kate Culhane: A Ghost Story*. The Hagues live in Colorado Springs, Colorado.

"Nicely updated version of Potter's charming tale."
—*Library Talk*

"Hague's illustrations . . . set a dark and theatrical mood." —*Kirkus Reviews*